JOSIE'S BUSY CALENDAR

WRITTEN BY
JENN WINT

ILLUSTRATED BY
ALLISON ARNDT

EAST 26TH
PUBLISHING

For permissions requests, contact the publisher at www.east26thpublishing.com

Library of Congress Cataloging-in-Publication data is available
ISBN: (Hardback) 978-1-955077-19-4 | (Paperback) 978-1-955077-32-3 | (eBook) 978-1-955077-33-0

10 9 8 7 6 5 4 3 2 1
First printing edition 2021

East 26th Publishing
Houston, TX

www.east26thpublishing.com

FOR MICHELLE – MY LOUDEST CHEERLEADER

Josie was stuck at home and bored.
School ended and friends couldn't come over to play.

While both her parents worked from home, tapping
away at their computers, she tried to keep busy.

Music camp, soccer practice and theatre were all canceled.
Her calendar was empty, so she had to entertain herself.

At first it was fine keeping busy.
Josie had paint and sparkly markers
and created some unique works of art.

She had blocks that she used to create
magical worlds for whimsical characters.

She ate snacks while
she watched TV,

She timed herself running from
one end of the yard to the other,

And she kept close watch on Meow, the neighbor's sneaky cat.

MONTH
Clean Room
Pet Neighbor's Cat
SUN
MON
TUES
WED
THURS
FRI
SAT
Art class with Hug
Look for bugs
Paint with flowers from garden
Soccer practice
Music Camp.
Family Game Night!
Marcella's Birthday party
Yoga
Theatre
Yoga

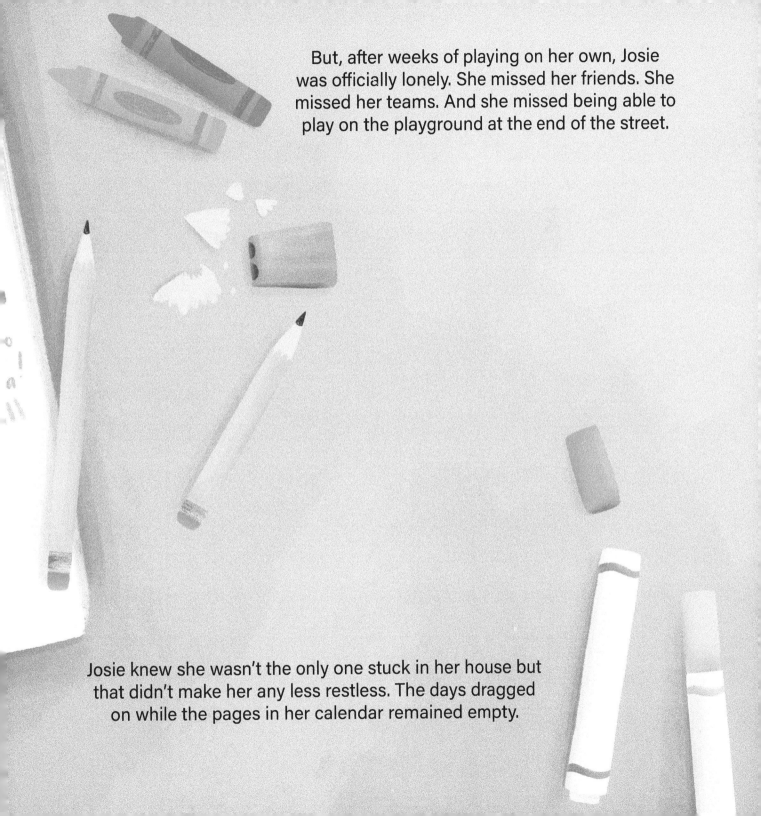

But, after weeks of playing on her own, Josie was officially lonely. She missed her friends. She missed her teams. And she missed being able to play on the playground at the end of the street.

Josie knew she wasn't the only one stuck in her house but that didn't make her any less restless. The days dragged on while the pages in her calendar remained empty.

Finally, one morning at breakfast Josie's Mom gave her the news she'd been waiting for. School was back open! The teachers would be giving lessons, games would be played, and best of all, most of her friends would be there!

On the first day back Josie was up early.
She had her breakfast eaten, teeth brushed and shoes
on before her Mom even asked. After playing alone for
so long she couldn't wait to be with her friends.

The first day of school was busy.
Everyone had stories about their time at home with their families.

Some kids had spent hours in the car driving to see grandparents.
Some had camped in remote places while others hadn't left the house at all.

Everyone agreed they had missed their friends and were glad to be back.

Josie didn't waste any time diving straight into lessons and gym class and art studio.

Now that she was allowed, she also set up some play dates!

By the end of the day, Josie had plans to play soccer with Liam on Monday, meet Drew at the playground on Tuesday and Marcella on Wednesday, bake with Nadia and Taylor on Thursday, ride bikes with Tilly on Friday, make posters with Rumi on Saturday and swim with Kelijah and Hugo on Sunday.

Her calendar was full!

MONT

SUN	MON	TUES	WED
4	5 Soccer with LIAM	PLAYGROUND WITH DREW 7	with MARC
11 SWIM WITH KeLIJAH AND HUGO	12	13 BUBBLe BaTH	14
18	19	20 ART cLaSS WITH HUGO	21

Soccer was great fun and it felt good to be back at the playground Tuesday and Wednesday but by Thursday Josie felt tired and restless.

Her tummy was in knots and she wasn't enjoying the chatter in her classroom as she had a few days earlier.

After school she asked Nadia and Taylor to bake without her and walked slowly towards her street, confused why her tummy was telling her to go home.

Josie was feeling anxious, but she didn't know why.

In the field by the playground, she stopped to rest.
Lying in the grass, she wondered what the crows were squawking about.
They hadn't had to stay home; they were always allowed to fly wherever they wanted.

Josie found herself wishing for her own black shiny wings.
She wished she could go back to the quiet days running laps in her
backyard and telling stories to the characters in her magical toy world.

She was confused why she didn't want to be baking with the friends she had been waiting to spend time with for so long.

As she took deep breaths and closed
her eyes, Josie let her mind wander.

She had missed play dates when she was
stuck at home but now that she was busy
with her friends, she missed being alone.

The knots in her tummy loosened as she
thought about how she was feeling.

Josie didn't want to be lonely, but she didn't like the feeling
that came when she rushed from one activity to the next.

She wondered if maybe she needed less things on her calendar?

What if, in order to balance her friends and herself
on her calendar, she counted herself as a friend?

Imagine that: being a friend to herself!

She decided then and there that a few days a week she
would schedule a play date with Josie to collect bugs and
practice her banjo. A bit of Josie-time would give her the
energy she needed to enjoy activities with her friends.

As she walked home, she passed the playground and waved
to her friends. They waved back and called her over.
Josie smiled but continued on her own.
Her tummy told her she should keep walking, so she listened.

MONTH

SUN	MON	TUES	WED	THURS	FRI	SAT
				1	2	3
4	5 Soccer with LIAM	6 PLAYGROUND with DREW	7 with MArcellA	8 BAKING with Nadia and TAYLOR	9 JOSIE TIME	10 Ma post wit
11 JOSIE TIME	12	13 BUBBLe BaTH	14	15	16	17
18	19	20	21 JOSIE TIME	22	23	
			28	29		JOSIE TIM

When she got home, Josie got out her calendar and wrote her own name on at least one day in every week with her favorite sparkly markers and sketched out the Josie adventures she was already planning.

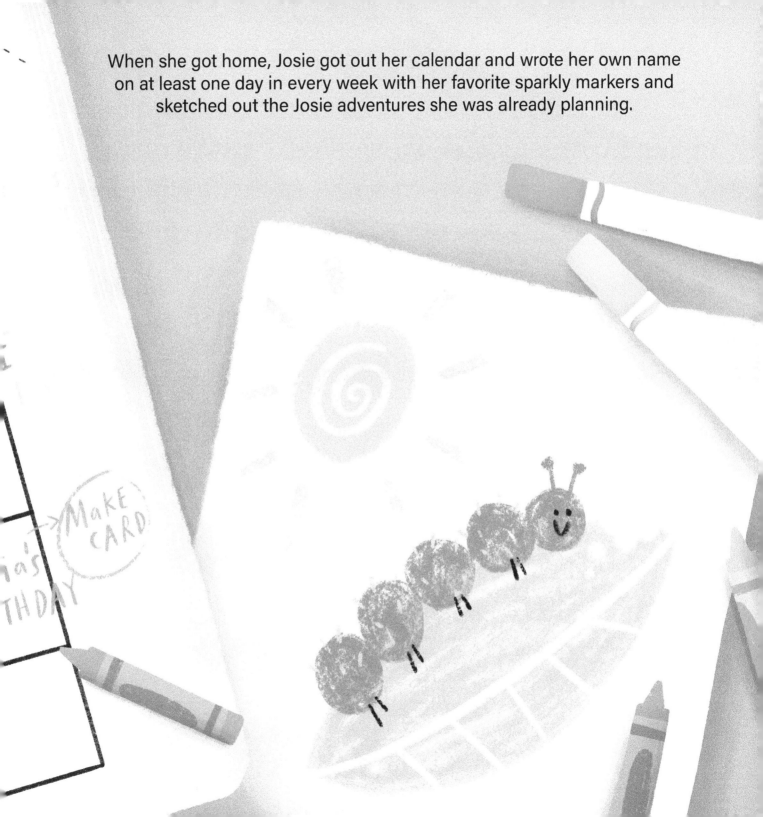

By the time Dad called her for dinner her tummy felt relaxed and hungry.

As Josie told her parents about her plan, she felt calm, and
looked forward to the following day's bike ride with Tilly, knowing
a break from busy and *time for herself* were written in her calendar.

AUTHOR JENN WINT

Jenn is a passionate and easily-inspired Public Relations & Communications specialist. She is the Founder of WINT Communications, regular contributor to VancouverMom.ca as well as mama to two littles and wife to an animated Irishman. Jenn suffered postpartum anxiety after the birth of her daughter and, in an attempt to explain her 'tummy knots' to her young son, began writing a children's book. After "post-pandemic anxiety" kicked in, she knew it was time to share this story with the world.

Jenn loves sharing the unique stories of brands she works with and is excited to tell her own stories through a fictional lens. She lives in Vancouver, Canada where she's on a continual quest to find the best chocolate chip cookie in the city.

To learn more about Jenn, you can find her on
Instagram and Twitter @jenn_wint
or visit her website at wintcommunications.com/books

CPSIA information can be obtained
at www.ICGtesting.com
Printed in the USA
LVHW070848170722
723692LV00011B/394

9 781955 077194